Cleveland Coxe

The Church and the Press

SALZWASSER
VERLAG

Cleveland Coxe

The Church and the Press

Reprint of the original, first published in 1859.

1st Edition 2022 | ISBN: 978-3-37513-226-2

Verlag (Publisher): Salzwasser Verlag GmbH, Zeilweg 44, 60439 Frankfurt, Deutschland
Vertretungsberechtigt (Authorized to represent): E. Roepke, Zeilweg 44, 60439 Frankfurt, Deutschland
Druck (Print): Books on Demand GmbH, In de Tarpen 42, 22848 Norderstedt, Deutschland

The Church and the Press:

OR,

CHRISTIAN LITERATURE
THE INHERITANCE OF THE CHURCH,

AND

THE PRESS AN EDUCATOR AND AN EVANGELIST.

A SERMON

PREACHED IN RICHMOND, AT ST. PAUL'S CHURCH, OCTOBER 12, 1859

AT THE

Eleventh Triennial Meeting of the S. S. Union and
Church Book Society.

BY A. CLEVELAND COXE,

Rector of Grace Church, Baltimore.

NEW-YORK:

General Protestant Episcopal S. S. Union and Church Book Society,

No. 762 BROADWAY.

1859.

SERMON.

" Moreover, because the Preacher was wise, he still taught the people knowledge." ECCLES. xii. 9.

THE policy of increasing religious knowledge by books of human authorship, originated with the wisest of mankind. He was a penman of the sacred oracles. In the dark sayings of his Proverbs, in the melody of his Canticles, and in the sublime morals of his Ecclesiastes, spake the Everlasting Word. But, of his own lofty enterprise, he was the father of the Hebrew literature. As such, he is the source to which the literature of Christians traces its majestic current. His works, as we learn elsewhere, were those of the moralist, the natural philosopher, and the poet. And in the context the Spirit of inspiration sets a seal to the inferior wisdom of his human authorship, in permitting him to say of it — " the Preacher sought to find out acceptable words!

and that which was written was upright, even words of truth." Such words, though uttered only by the written page, he invests with the character of sermons. They are, he affirms, "like goads and nails, fastened by the masters of assemblies;" like the pointed sayings and tenacious principles, driven into the consciences of great congregations, by masterly orators. Further, he argues, that all good words proceed from the "one Shepherd" and Bishop of souls, the Word of God. Moreover, while he anticipates the objection that "much study is a weariness to the flesh," and that "of making many books there is no end," he yet exhorts the young to be instructed by such words as prepare the soul for duty and for judgment. In this way, the royal author seems to vindicate his own title of "the Preacher;" and we infer the principle that good books are great preachers.

The Society which has made me its advocate is the Institution of a past generation. It is already venerable and historical, as owing its existence to eminent divines and *preachers* who have passed away. "By it, they being dead, yet speak;" and "because they were wise, they still teach the people knowledge." I present the claims of a Christian press, of tried usefulness, but entirely unendowed, and not too liberally sup-

ported. I shall endeavour to persuade you that
it ought to be promoted to the front rank of our
aggressive agencies; that, on a greatly enlarged
scale of operation, it should be brought to bear
upon the educated mind of our countrymen,
and upon the mind which is now in process of
education : and first of all, I shall try to show
that, for the present crisis at least, while we
lack living preachers, we must make the Press
a missionary, and trust to it, under God, as our
grand resource.

In urging this consideration, that the Christian press is a missionary, and may be made
the instrument of multiplying indefinitely the
voices and energies of your existing missionaries,
I feel that I have a great advantage in the time
and order of my appeal. I follow the stirring
addresses and sermons of fathers and brethren
who have warmed your hearts, and enlarged
them to the vastness and glory of the missionary
work. Powerfully have they impressed you
with a view of the destitution, the unbelief,
the utter irreligion of many parts of our land.
Where are the preachers ? Lord Jesus—send
forth labourers ! But, till this cry is answered
are we to do nothing ? I read that "wisdom
strengtheneth the wise more than ten mighty
men ;" and I urge the counsel of the Preacher

to teach Christian knowledge and wisdom by books and tracts. These are the goads and nails which for the present must be pointed and fastened upon the minds of our countrymen. I claim, then, for my subject something of that devout interest with which you have listened to appeals in behalf of Missions. I speak in the same cause; I plead for the means to multiply the energies and the achievements of your pastors and evangelists.

I fear that, as a Church, we have underestimated the Press: I am sure we have not sufficiently employed it: I feel that we ought to wake up to the wealth of our literary resources, and to the power we might exert by bringing them out, and making them known and felt. True, nothing can supply the place of the living preacher; the steward of Christ's mysteries; the ambassador of heaven : and we are justly jealous of those exaggerated eulogies of the Press, which are popular, because they flatter souls in the delusive idea that they may spare themselves the pains of communion with the Church, and be scriptural Christians by reading good books, in their own houses. Besides, we have seen, in our day, such abuses of the Press as beget reactionary fears. Hence, many seem to have a feeling that the Press is a creature which " is not subject to the law of God, neither indeed can be." They tremble at the infidel vaunt, which implies that the invention of the Press was a surprise upon Providence itself; that it is an engine which the Author of the Gospel took not into account; an instrument which is to undermine and explode the Faith of Ages. And true it is, that the Press of our country suggests cause for anxiety and alarm. It already battens upon popular vice and passion. It is made a tremendous agent of corruption. By night and day, by the untiring energy of steam, and as it were with the very flame of Tophet, it sends forth elements of pollution, the most corrosive. One is tempted to think that the Spirit of prophecy spake of this mechanical tongue, rather than of that which is the glory of our frame, when He said— "It is a fire; a world of iniquity; it setteth on fire the course of nature, and it is set on fire of hell."

But bad as the tongue is, what are we to do with it? "Awake up, my glory! I will give praise with the best member that I have." This same tongue which cannot be tamed by man, is tamed by God. His Holy Spirit makes it a flame of Pentecost; a world of illumination and of blessing. Now the law of the tongue must be the law of the press: for what is the press

but an instrument of utterance? Words are
their common product; and written words like
spoken words, when they are good, are declared
by Solomon to be of the nature of sermons.
God employs the tongues of good men to confound the Babel-builders of irreligion; and so
he can employ a Christian press to overpower
the printing of the wicked. For there is, and
ever has been, a supernatural law as to words;
a law of Providence which restrains those over-
flowings of ungodliness, which would otherwise
deluge the world. "The fruit of the lips" is a
harvest of which God takes care that he shall
have the increase. Humanly speaking it would
be impossible that the words of a few fishermen
should prevail over the words of all the world
besides: but the unseen Spirit has made them
infinitely superior to all the " enticing words of
man's wisdom." And so, while the heathen
rage, the words of the gospel go on to perpetual
mastery. The servants of Christ may seem to
imitate their dear Master, and neither strive nor
cry, nor lift up their voice in the streets; yet
says the proverb, " The words of the wise are
heard in quiet more than the outcry of him that
ruleth among fools." Voltaire and Rousseau
make a great noise in their generation; nations
become fools and enthrone them as rulers; but

there is such a thing as " the blasting of the breath of the displeasure of Jehovah." Their words are smitten with anathema; their triumphing is short, for it is necessarily the triumph of destructiveness and blood. The charter of a Christian press runs parallel with that law of God—"The lip of Truth shall be established forever: but a lying tongue is but for a moment."

Let us recognize the Press, then, as the gift of God : the earnest of his gracious promise that in the last days "knowledge shall be increased." Take its actual history.[a] For four centuries it has been yielding its steady tribute to Truth. No wonder that the same enemy that sowed tares with the good seed of the word, has made mischief here also : but the harvest is the Lord's, and so is that vintage which this press turns into the new wine of Pentecost. What is called the invention of printing, is rather its Epiphany ; its manifestation. God made it " beautiful in its time." Men understood the principle long before.[b] The ancients used seals and dies. The bakers and plumbers of Pompeii printed their names on loaves of bread, and leaden pipes. The major and the minor were not wanting : but God would not let the active mind of man complete the syllogism, till all things were ready.

[a] See Note A.   [b] See Note B.

The promise was that when many should run to and fro, then knowledge should be commensurately increased. At length, this new era was at hand. After long darkness—the dry land of this great continent was about to appear. It was then that God said "Let there be light;" and when thousands took the wings of the morning and fled to these uttermost parts of the earth, they were able to bring with them, in printed Bibles, the blessed assurance that even here His hand should hold, and His right hand sustain.

Printing was the gift of God to his Church—the angel that knocked off the manacles from the Gospel, and brought St. Peter again out of prison, to feed Christ's sheep; to feed His lambs. Yet its power for doing evil was foreseen from the beginning. As Friar Bacon is said to have strangled the monster gunpowder, with conscientious alarm, in the moment when the flash of his crucible announced its birth, so John Guttemberg had great searchings of heart, with respect to his portentous discovery. In the cloisters of Arbogasta, a spirit passed before him, and tempted him in the guise of an angel of light.[c] It said—"John Guttemberg, thou hast made thy name immortal, but ah! at what a price! Bethink thee, what thou art doing. The ungodly are many more than the good: thy work will but

[c] See Note C.

multiply their blasphemies and lies. Thou hast uncovered the bottomless pit. Henceforth a swarm of seducing spirits shall come forth like the brood of Abaddon, and make the earth a hell. Oh, think of millions of souls corrupted by thine exploit: the venom of fiends distilled into the souls of tender maidens, and boys made old by it, in the experience of sin! See mothers weeping over their demoniac sons, and gray-haired fathers hiding their faces from the shame of daughters. Yes! even the young virgin will be seduced to read what she would never have listened to; and thy press shall be the pander of lust. Destroy it, John! Forget thy monstrous conception: forbear, by multiplying the resources of the wicked, to make thyself, throughout all ages, the partner of their crimes." From such a dream John Guttemberg awoke, and no marvel that he trembled! He was on the point of burying his secret in oblivion; as the genie in the Arabian tale shrank back into its casket, and was engulfed by the hand that had enlarged it. But—"I reflected," says the sublime discoverer, "that the gifts of God, though often perilous, are never bad. I saw that to endow intelligence with such a faculty was to open fresh fields to wisdom and to goodness, both alike divine. I proceeded with my discovery."

Thank God, he did so ! First of all, he printed the first Psalm ; a prophecy of success to " the man who hath not walked in the counsel of the un-godly, nor sat in the seat of the scornful." It promised that " his leaf shall not wither," but that " as for the ungodly, it is not so with them, but they are like the chaff which the wind scattereth away." Such was the charter of the Press, in the day when the Lord God created it. He made it very good. He laid his hand upon it, and ordained it: he bade it be fruitful and mul-tiply, and replenish the earth ; and lo ! its first utterance proclaimed freedom to the fettered Scriptures. Its next voice was the Reformation.

And shall the Church of God fail to recognise His call to use this noble augmentation of her faculties in proportion as ungodly men abuse it? All the evil of which its inventor dreamed, is a practical fact in this land. Mechanical powers and agencies of which he had no idea have made manifold all the mischief suggested by his vision. What then ? So much louder is the cry to the Church, to confound them by the same machinery. Remember, that Guttemberg and Columbus were men of the same times ; the Press was provided for America ; it was an in-strument absolutely essential to the rapid civil-ization of this continent. And shall the Church fail to use it ? Let no man suggest our scanty resources, in contrast with those of the ungodly. There is a divine machinery working for and with the children of light, of which the men of this world, who are so " wise in their genera-tion," fail to take account. Ezekiel saw it by the river Chebar. The breath of the living crea-ture was in it. It had—

" Wheel within wheel revolving :"

"and as for the wheels, they went, every one, straight forward."

Such are some of our encouragements to econ-omize the Press, on a new and noble scale. I suggest another, by appealing to all who hear me. What do you not owe to impressions re-ceived from printed books ? Where and what would you have been, but for pious reading ? What would tempt you to part with your little hoard of precious volumes ? To say nothing of the origin of religious feeling, in thousands of cases, is it not true that books have been the recruiting-sergeants of our Church and Ministry ? Is it not a fact that among the fathers and brethren here present, in this great council of our Church, there are not a few who are in-debted to the silent testimony of books for their first knowledge of her ways of pleasantness and paths of peace ?[d]

d See Note D.

The important epochs in our progress as a
Church, have been those of increased activity in
publishing ; of bringing forth our treasures, new
and old.   For a long time almost our only allies
were the booksellers.   Schools and colleges were
in the possession of others : but men could not
reprint nor sell the standard works of English
literature without being our helpers ; for that literature is born of the Church, its own begotten
child.   On this significant and inspiring consideration, permit me for a moment to enlarge.

It is said of Solomon : "God gave him wisdom
and understanding, exceeding much, and large-
ness of heart, even as the sand that is by the
seashore."   No wonder then that the text goes
on to tell how religion received from him a hand-
maid in Polite Learning, and that he gave Science
to be a servant honourable in all her house.
At the same time that the mind of Greece, and
of her colonies, was turning as wax to the seal to-
ward the genius of Homer, and accepting as a sort
of Bible those bewitching rhapsodies which recognized "lords many and gods many," and which
enthroned them as tutelary principalities over
woods and streams, and fountains and great
deeps, and lofty mountains—this wise Hebrew,
barred out, as it were, the contagion of idolatry
by creating for his countrymen, a literature

which recognized Jehovah, and crowned Him only, as Sovereign of His own universe. In the Song of the Three Children, and in other portions of the Apocrypha, I suspect we have the remnants and translations of what originally proceeded from him. He was the greatest author of his times. "His fame was in all nations round about; and he spake three thousand proverbs; and his songs were a thousand and five; and he spake of trees, from the cedar that is in Lebanon, even unto the hyssop that springeth out of the wall; he spake also of beasts, and of fowl, and of creeping things, and of fishes."

Ours is a day of godless science, and our children are constantly exposed to the influences of a popular authorship, which certainly is not devout. The general half-learning of our countrymen is singularly inclined to that spirit which would banish God from his own creation, and which would reverse the law—" let God be true and every man a liar." Hence arises the suggestion that we owe it to ourselves to create a national literature, in the spirit of Solomon's enterprise. But, I forbear to dwell on this idea, because it is not a practical one. We cannot vote such a literature into existence. God gives genius to whom he will, and it must be his glorious endowment if ever the Church becomes the mistress of the national intellect, and so insures a healthful literature to our country. At present, a sickly sentimentality, a meagre rationalism, a mean provincialism, threaten to debase what true religion alone can ennoble. American books are too generally made for the million, and pander to the most degrading prejudices. They flatter Popery and fawn on Infidelity at the same moment. Beware of such books—" Encyclopædias," " Popular Libraries," " Family Periodicals." Banish them from your homes. Encourage such authors as have aimed to give a healthful tone to popular thought. Estimate aright what we owe to those eminent popular authors of our own Communion, who, while they do honour to their country, manifest that elevated enthusiasm for the Church, which the use of the English language ought to inspire.° Let such examples give us hope for the future ; but meantime, let us reflect that the stores of English literature are the patrimony of the Church, and that the wholesome supplies, which at this moment are teeming from the press of our mother Church may be lawfully reproduced and appropriated. What a resource is here ! It is our own fault if the youth of the Nation, and our children in particular, are reared at the feet of a godless Science, or compelled to learn history and every-

° See Note E.

thing else that is useful to the mind, under the ferule of a rigid Puritanism, or of a Rationalism that is its next of kin, and which, like it, distorts and disqualifies and degrades whatever it takes in hand.[f]

Let us not forget that the task of Solomon has been taken into commission by the great worthies of our own Church, in past times. Our children may be readily initiated in the study of Nature, in the reverent spirit of Bacon, of Boyle, and of Newton. There have been many like John Evelyn to "speak of trees." White of Selborne discourses charmingly of " beasts and fowl and creeping things ;" and who knows not how the pious Walton, whose every line is baited with a moral, has " spoken of fishes ?" Then for "songs," how rich and various is the pure poetry of our language from that of Spenser and Herbert, to that of Cowper and Southey and Wordsworth ; glittering names in the firmament of genius, and stars, I doubt not, in the Paradise of God ! Happy, indeed, is the household where the piety of youth is matured by a genial fellowship with minds like these ; minds of the first order, themselves the nurslings of the Church's breast.[g] Shall we fail, then, to make it felt by our countrymen, that such works as theirs are the fruitage of those tough old roots—

[f] See Note F.　　　　　[g] See Note G.

the Catechism and the Liturgy? Is it not
policy, wisdom, duty, to teach our countrymen
that this old wine is better than the new?
And in view of the fact that everywhere a pesti-
lent press is multiplying among us a yellow and
cadaverous literature which is fit only for Sodom
and Gomorrah; or reproducing that which
comes reeking with fumes of stale debauch from
France and Germany; is it not time for us to
direct attention, in every way, to the sweet and
wholesome sources of mental aliment, which I
have indicated as our own? Oh, the delicious
fragrance of our old-fashioned Christian literature;
the literature of which no gentleman can be
ignorant, without disgrace;[h] and which, in its
secondary forms is as useful to the common
mind, as to that which is refined! An ennobling
history which nobody can read without conscious elevation of thought and feeling, is part
of it.[i] Its poetry and its romance are pure.[j] Our
children may safely enjoy its fragrance, which
is as the scent of fields in June. No serpent is
coiled under its flowers; its symbol is Naphtali's
"hind let loose;" a glad creature of God, as it
bounds through glade and forest; whose every
motion inspireth, and in that sense "giveth
goodly words."

My argument suggests the inference that in

h See Note H.   i See Note I.   j See Note J.

the formation of Parochial and Domestic Libraries, I would by no means limit the selection to our theological literature, incomparable and precious as it is.[k] But, I pass to a brief review of the vast benefits we have already derived, from a policy inaugurated more than a century ago, on the banks of the fair river, which, at this moment, seems to mingle the murmur of its waters, with that of our counsels and brotherly debates. Here, in the Old Dominion, and under the hoary walls of Jamestown, were read those inspiring allegories which Spenser[l] dedicated to Elizabeth as "Empresse of Virginia." Our colonial clergy brought out books with them, and established lending-libraries. Let Virginia remember the name of Blair. Let the name of Commissary Bray be uttered with a fervour of gratitude, for perhaps the largest share of that wisdom and benevolence which founded the " Society for the Promotion of Christian Knowledge ;" for the zeal which brought him to one of these Southern provinces, laden with gifts and bounties; and for the generous foresight, which endowed us with books of sound divinity and science. Who can tell how much this ungrateful nation, ever forgetful of moral benefits and benefactors, owes, at least indirectly, to him ? Reflect that from the means which he and his associates supplied

[k] See Note K.   [l] See Note L,

was derived the education of Washington and
his illustrious contemporaries.[m]

To Bishop Berkeley's policy in sending a noble
library to Yale College, may be traced much of
the intelligent piety of New England.[n]   But
books had been missionaries before him, and by
their silent preaching had already turned the
President and leading scholars of that Puritan
university into Churchmen.   So, books may be
said to have laid the foundations of the Church
in New England, the vaunted inheritance of her
hereditary foes.   In all ages books have won
our greatest trophies.   Our cause languishes
only when it is in the keeping of dullness and
indifference.   It invokes light : it challenges
investigation.   Our great reformers worked the
press, as if it had been the artillery of England.
Then came Jewel, and Hooker, and Field, with
their broadsides against Papists and Puritans;
and when John Milton brought his erratic genius to the aid of the latter, it was with the
damaging confession that the Bishops' books
were better and more learned than those of their
adversaries, who had not been equal to the con-
test.[o]   This patronizing office of championship
involved even Milton in defeat.   In his theology
the poet is " shorn of his beams."   His argument against prelacy is a fit companion for that
which he produced in favour of polygamy.

[m] See Note M.   [n] See Note N.   [o] See Note O.

For a time, and till the dreary tyranny of
Cromwell was overpast, it was almost to
books alone that we owed, under God, the
unquenched coal of the Church, which glowed
on English hearth-stones. The "Whole Duty
of Man" preached its homely sermons, by the
lips of pious mothers; and in many a cottage and
hall, it was for long years the only pastor ever-
seen or heard. Then, too, were wrought those
apples of gold in pictures of silver—the " Life of
Christ," and the "Golden Grove" of our Anglican Chrysostom: and then how mightily came
forth the sun of the Church's strength, and with
what redoubled radiance, in the works of those
brilliant scholars and divines that illustrated the
otherwise gloomy days, extending from the pri-
macy of Juxon to that of Sancroft! Nor should
we forget that when a frigid latitudinarianism
had set in, like a cold noon after a fine spring morning, it was to books and masterly tracts, to the
works of such as Butler, and Waterland, and
Jones of Nayland, and Bishop Horne, that we
owe, under Providence, the unchanging fidelity
of Anglican theology, to the cardinal truths of
revelation ; to the doctrines of the divinity and
atonement of Christ, and of our justification by
faith in His precious blood.[p] I appeal to you,
venerable fathers and dear brethren in the minis-

p See Note P.

try, is it not by contact with such minds that many of you first learned to know the love of Christ, and to choose the blessed work of preaching His gospel ? Have they not been to thousands as the hem of the Saviour's garment, through which virtue went out of Him to heal them ? Why, then, do we forbear to bring all intelligent minds in our country into such contact? Why do we leave the hints which experience has given us unimproved ? Why do we not develope our vast resources by the Press, and force them upon the attention of the times ? In spite of themselves, men who aim at a high cultivation must know something of our great divines ; and to this fact we owe, in no small degree, the steady influx of educated mind into the ranks of our ministry.[q] Why, then, I say, is not every college and fireside in our land, forced by our energy and forethought to feel, and pay tribute to such lawful claims ? We have no right to withhold knowledge. Give inquiring men, at least, the chance to understand and reject our theology. But thousands would never reject it, if only they might know of it. Why should they live and die in ignorance of what to us is dearer than life itself ? Oh, that I could adequately express my convictions of our duty in this matter ! Was ever a church so rich in re-

[q] See Note Q.

sources and so slow to use them : so full of light and so cruelly unwilling to let her light shine ?

Observe, how the policy of our opponents betrays the point in which they feel themselves weak, and in which they dread our power. How instinctively the colleges of New England have shrunk from encouraging the study of English literature, sacred and secular! How unconsciously they have conceded that to make young men drink deep of these undefiled wells, would be to disgust them with extemporaneous devotions, and create a longing for the sublime old Liturgy! How unfortunate has been their alternative, in the importation of German rationalism into all their schools! And how rapidly the decline of public morals, of the dignity of personal bearing, and of thought and speech accordingly,[r] has warned us to beware ; and invoked us to bring forth our candle from under its bushel !

Not less instinctively does the Romanist dread the influence of the literature which I am commending. Next to the Scriptures, he recognizes it as the most formidable fortress in which the Anglo-Saxon intellect entrenches itself against him. Well he may: for it arose with Wiclif and Chaucer, and stands an enduring witness that " righteousness exalteth a nation." Happily this identity of English literature with pure

[r] See Note R.   [s] See Note S.

religion can never be destroyed. To seduce the
youth of England, the Romanists lately founded
an university in the sister isle. That baleful genius who led the apostasy from Oxford to Rome
tried to show them that if they would make their
pupils a match for the scholars of Oxford and
Cambridge, they must imbue them, as scholars,
with the same literature; and he urged them to
make the experiment, with all the powers of his
persuasive eloquence.[t] But no—his superiors
decided that it was too bold an experiment. English literature, they argued, must breed Anglican
churchmen. They barred their doors against it.
Be it so; but let us learn from the enemy a great
secret of successful war! Yes, my brother
Churchman, use what they concede to you; recognize your superiority; know your strength;
know that to train your children faithfully in
the language which their mothers speak, is to
imbue them with healthful religion; is to make
them hate a lie; is to give them an habitual hos-
tility to superstition. Yes—it is to endow them
with a mental manhood, to which they must do
degrading violence before they can alienate
themselves from her whose maternal bosom has
seldom lost a child of its nurture, that was not
hopelessly ignoble in taste, or fanatical in tem-
perament.

[t] See Note T.

Considerations such as these convince me, that the Society whose claims I urge may be made by ample support an instrument of good, almost in any degree you may choose. It may be made a voice in the wilderness to prepare the way of the Lord. It will bring in recruits for the ministry, from all parts of the land. It will make its way where the foot of a Churchman never falls ; it will win the sweet confidence of good men, who have found the bitterest disappointment in the ministry of other communions ; it will penetrate into the nurseries of children. And when the missionary's visit to the lonely outpost has come to an end, it will enable him to leave supplies of Sunday reading, till after a long time he shall come again to seek the sheep that else would have been lost. Surely our books are needed everywhere in the land; from Maine, where its good prelate has been obliged so lately to tell them that there is a devil, to Oregon, where its bold apostle has oftentimes to remind them that there is a God.

I know that there is a great circulation in this land, of books that are vaguely Christian, and indefinitely religious: but, remember, Churchmen, that, without forgetting to be grateful for what is done by others, your books are the only ones that venture to set forth the entire truth as

it is in Jesus : the New Testament in its integ-
rity : the whole counsel of God.   All this, our
Mixed Societies do not profess to do : their organ-
ization forbids it : they cannot, on their plan of
action, even undertake to expound the six " principles of the doctrine of Christ," as enumerated
by St. Paul.ᵘ   I exhort you then, not interfering
with them, to do your own proper work ; to econo-
mize your own resources ; to endow and enrich
and energize your own Society.   Let it no
l onge drag in the rear ; let it go hand
in hand with your great missionary agencies :
enlarge its gratuitous issues.   Take of it
for your own families ; but give others also to
drink.   Thousands are thirsting for the truth
that lies in our well.   To drop the figure, there
is a turning to our Church, among the most
earnest minds in the land, and a longing to learn
of us, how to escape from the miseries and dis-
tractions of a divided Christianity.   Oh, that
we may prove ourselves worthy of being thus
" sought out—a city not forsaken."   Let us arise
to the measure of these responsibilities.   Let our
presses burst out with new wine, of the old flavour;
let our books go everywhere preaching the word.
Establish depositories in every city ; open libraries in every parish; send out hawkers; wake up
fathers of families to the duty of providing

ᵘ See Note U.

bread for their children's minds; and let mothers learn not only that book-shelves are the fairest ornaments of a dwelling, but that " through wisdom is a house builded, and by knowledge shall the chambers be filled with all precious and pleasant riches."

Finally, to fasten in a sure place the rude intelligence of your backwoodsmen, supply the frontier missionary with these " goads and nails." Do this, and I will venture to sketch in the outline the results, which facts already established enable us to anticipate as probable.[v] The lad that, in some western cabin, pores over stories that illustrate the Catechism, is the predestined apostle of Utah — the Antipas (the faithful martyr, possibly) who is to reclaim to decency and the fear of God its unhappy progeny of lust and crime. Or perhaps, the intelligent boy, who, of a cold winter night, in Minnesota, shall explore, by the blazing fire on the hearth, the story of Latimer and Ridley, may be leaning on the little hand that is yet to light new candles of Reformation, and wrest back the fairest domains of the Mississippi, from the grasp of Romish superstition and imposture. Or it may be, when we too shall have passed away and left our places to others, that the element of your Society shall be found to have nurtured the

[v] See Note V.

man—that special gift of God, for whose appear
ance millions of prayers are daily sent up to
His throne by Christians of different names—
the man who, in these last days, must be raised
up, to turn the hearts of fathers to their children, and of children to their fathers: to gather
all believers in America into the one fold, under
one Shepherd; and to unite the now divided
Christians of our beloved country into one Sac-
ramental host, able to confront all "the armies
of the aliens," and to fill this continent with
the voice of one triumphant ascription: "Worthy is the Lamb."

NOTES.

AT the request of several of the officers and friends of the Church Book Society, the author appends a series of notes, designed to give a more detailed and practical shape to the brief suggestions of the sermon. He does this, deeply impressed with the importance of the matters on which he touches, but with no idea that he advances anything which many have not thought of before. He hopes to be serviceable, however, to men of business, fathers of families, and others who will give the Sermon the honour of a reading, but who may *have no time* to elaborate for themselves opinions and practical operations in harmony with its counsels.

Hundreds, if not thousands of Churchmen, visit New-York every year, who make the purchase of books for their families part of their errand, but in the excitement of their business and pleasure, they are not able to give the selection of proper books a moment's thought. Naming a few popular authors, they often leave the rest to an incompetent bookseller, with orders to put up a parcel, at a specified price : as the result, they receive, if not a mass of refuse merchandise, at least an indiscriminate pile of showy but often ill-assorted books, many of them entirely unfit for a Christian's household shelves. The books they ought to possess they never see ; their children never hear of them ; and yet even a little money, judiciously laid out in books, goes a great way, and a few well-selected volumes give an air of dignity and taste to the humblest home, while even the familiar sight of their titles does much to enlarge and liberalize the minds of the young.

United action among Churchmen, in behalf of their own literary wants, would soon compel authors and publishers to desist from doing continual outrage to their principles. We need a recognized literary policy. An outline of the kind of reading we require is furnished in these notes, and it seems desirable that, when this outline is properly filled up, the Society should issue a list of such books as it is willing to procure for parties buying its own publications, with a view to promote healthful tastes, and such *habits of thought* as coincide with the principles of Churchmen. The Church finds no greater barrier to her progress than the vulgar tastes, prejudices, and ways of viewing things in general, which are produced by the provincial and low-lived literature that is current in the land.

A.

The Actual History of the Press. Dean Milman, in his " Latin Christianity," says of the era of printing : " Books gradually became, as far as the instruction of the human race, *a co-ordinate priesthood.*"

B.

The Principle of Printing always known. The Chinese, of course, claim this invention, and date it before the Christian era. Cicero often uses language and imagery which one would imagine sufficient to suggest the art of printing to any one. Thus : " Quid si in ejusdemmodi cera centum sigilla hoc annulo impressero ?" IV. Acad., 85. Again : " An imprimi, quasi ceram, animum putamus, et memoriam esse signatarum rerum in mente vestigia ? Quæ possunt verborum, quæ rerum ipsarum, esse vestigia ? Quæ porro tam immensa magnitudo, quæ illa tam multa possit effingere ?" Tusc. I., 25.

C.

Guttemberg's Vision. I have taken the liberty to tell this story in my own language, but those who would see it more dramatically drawn out, are referred to the spirited narrative of M. de Lamartine, *Vie des Grands Hommes*, vol. ii., p. 122.

D.

Influence of Books. Here, if the preacher speaks feelingly, he speaks from precious experience. To Mrs. Sherwood's *Stories on the Church Catechism* (afterwards edited by Bishop Kemp), he owes the blessed privilege of having been instructed in the Catechism of the Church, while yet a child in the nursery, and in the tones of a mother's voice. Though familiar with the Services of the Church, from tender years, circumstances obliged him to depend upon books, in a large measure, for education in her principles. The History of England, and the Lives of her martyrs and great divines, and of Henry Martyn, and Reginald Heber, not forgetting the Memoirs and Correspondence of William Cowper, Hannah More, and Leigh Richmond, served to enamour him with their several types of Anglican character and piety, long before he could understand the importance of doctrinal orthodoxy. To *The Records of a Good Man's Life, The Rectory of Valehead, Scenes in our Parish*, and several other works of similar spirit, he owed, in a great degree, a prevailing reverence and love for our holy religion, during a perilous period of boyhood. In early college-life he was induced, by the advice of a Presbyterian scholar, to study the History of Canonical Scripture, in the learned work of (the Dissenter) Jeremiah Jones—a work which has been thought worthy of publication by the Oxford University Press. To this work he owes his first insight of the Primitive Church, and of the clear truth that the Orders of the Church are derived from the same sources which supply us with the sacred Scriptures. This truth, as he thus grasped it, he has endeavoured to illustrate in the little brochure entitled " Fixed Principles."

E.

Popular Authors among American Churchmen. It need hardly be said that the works of Washington Irving, J. Fenimore Cooper, and others, are here referred to. The writings of Mr. Irving are pre-eminently entitled to such commendation. In a striking manner they show what English genius naturally becomes, under the influence of the Church in a new country, and under new institutions; hence they are legitimate and healthful grafts upon the old English stock. They *keep up the literary succession* between America and the old English writers, which, but for Mr. Irving, would hardly be apparent. Hence, a taste for Irving's works leads a young mind up to the sources of the language, and fosters an intellectual habit, which nothing less than the Church and her Liturgy can satisfy. He is the father of Polite Letters in America. Mr. Cooper, though in a less degree, perhaps (yet at times even more conspicuously), has woven into his works a large amount of Anglican thought and expression. As time goes on, the merits of "The Pioneers," and its kindred tales, will be more and more appreciated. The "Rural Hours" of Miss Cooper is a charming work; and "The American Lady," by Mrs. Grant, of Laggan, should be read with Mr. Cooper's stories, by all who would gain a true idea of some of the earlier phases of life in this western world.

P. S.—This note was written almost at the very hour when the amiable and accomplished Mr. Irving was expiring at Irvington— an event for which nobody was prepared. In the general attention which will now be directed to his writings, Churchmen have an opportunity to enforce the views here presented, and which the writer has more fully illustrated in the "Church Review," vol. iii., p. 344. It may be worth stating that Mr. Irving was much gratified with the view of his influence on Church development there presented.

F.

Puritanized Histories. Of this ignoble sort is even tne work (which aspires to be a national one) of Mr. Bancroft. Happily, it cannot be read by youth with any such enthusiasm as will always be inspired by Irving's Washington. A History of America, divested of sectional prejudices, and illustrating the rise of our civilization, literature, and arts, remains to be written. The colonial period has never been carefully treated; and the squalid politics of the nation, subsequent to the formation of our constitution, may well be thrown into the shade by some historian who will do justice to the amazing development of society under the Presidents.

Of the Plymouth colony a fair and interesting memoir has been written by one of our own clergy, the Rev. A. Steele, of Washington, entitled "The Chief of the Pilgrims." To Professor Eliot, of Trinity College, we are also indebted for a Manual of American History which deserves notice.

G.

Suggestion. The popular work, *Chambers' Encyclopædia of English Literature,* is worthy of a place in a family library. On the whole, it is an excellent introduction to the noble study here recommended, and can hardly fail of inspiring the youthful mind, that is otherwise well trained, with a love of letters. The author takes pleasure in recording a general impression in favour of the similar work of the Messrs. Duyckinck, on American literature.

H.

Safe Guides. I beg to direct attention to the writings of the late Professor Reed, of the University of Pennsylvania, as of great value in education, and worthy of the sound Churchman and devout Christian who has left them to us. I refer especially to his *Lectures on English Literature,* and his *Lectures on English History ;* the latter founded on Shakspeare. I would also refer the reader to Mr. Hudson's *Lectures on Shakspeare,* as full of valuable comment. Nor can I forbear to mention the names of William Croswell, Bishop Doane, James Hillhouse, Edward Griffin, and James Wallis Eastburn, among those of our benefactors, in forming the literary tastes of Churchmen. Let me not omit Dr. Jarvis, and Bishop Wainwright.

I.

Historic Studies. As an introduction to English Church History, I cannot too warmly commend Mr. Southey's *Book of the Church ;* but it must be regarded merely as an introduction. He wrote before much attention had been given to many of the more important points of our history, as specialties, and hence allowance must be made for inaccuracies of statement and of expression, of which the correction will be found in such works as Massingberd's *History of the English Reformation,* Churton's *Early English Church,* and Le Bas' *Lives of Wiclif, Cranmer, and Laud.* Besides these, Palgrave's *Truths and Fictions of the Middle Ages,* and the same author's *Anglo-Saxons,* should be read.

In pursuing this all-important study—all-important, because it is by such studies that character is elevated, and emancipated from what is provincial, contracted, and false—*The Church History of Britain,* by Fuller, may next be taken up. It will never be laid down for long, by anybody who loves a genuine repast of wit, a flow of good tempered but epigrammatic criticism, a fund of entertaining anecdote, and a genial vein of piety withal, though not unflavored with a tart prickliness at times, owing to the author's sympathy with the better sort of Puritans. After this one may take up, successively, Lord Clarendon's *History of the Rebellion,* and Burnet's *History of His Own Times,* though it would be better to begin with his *History of the Reformation.* In all such writers allowance must be made for their prejudices ; in Burnet, for something like misrepresentation, besides frequent inaccuracy. The *Biography of Charles the First,* by Mr. D'Israeli, is a very valuable work in its way, but the times of that sovereign must be studied from original sources, by every American who would understand the period to which the history of his own country is most deeply and vitally related. It is a study in which every jurist and divine, more especially, should be thoroughly well read.

There are side-dishes to this great feast which must not be forgotten. Taking it for granted that a youth will have made himself familiar with the historical plays of Shakspeare, and Chaucer's Prologue to the Canterbury Tales, I would advise him to resort to the *Paston Letters*, and to read the *Colloquies of Erasmus* (translated by L'Estrange), in order to get hold of the times preceding the Reformation, in their manners and customs. Then read *Wotton's Reliquiæ*, Howell's *Familiar Letters*, and Walton's *Lives*, and the *Complete Angler*. Sir Thomas Herbert's *Two Last Years of Charles the First*, though an authentic personal memoir, has all the charm of romance. The *Diary and Letters of John Evelyn*, and (as a contrast partly) the *Diary of Pepys*, are also of great interest; they supply important facts, and Evelyn teaches us the manners of a true, old-fashioned, Christian gentleman, all the more forcibly, when set off by the garrulous coxcomb whose life runs so nearly parallel. Fuller's " Worthies," and Burnet's *Lives* (edited by Jebb) should not be forgotten ; nor can I forbear to throw in Sir Thomas Brown's *Religio Medici,* and Selden's *Table-talk ;* the latter because it teaches us to understand and do justice to those of the Puritans who differed least from the Church. After this may be read, as *historical* works, the Spectator, and then Boswell's Johnson. Horace Walpole's gossip gives a melancholy, but to some extent, a truthful picture of the times, of which Dr. Johnson enables us to see the redeeming features. With those times our own colonial history is closely connected. Dr. Hook's *Ecclesiastical Biography* ought to be newly edited and re-published, with additions, in America : and this work, with the estimable Dr. Sprague's *Annals of the American Pulpit*, (vol. IV.,) will materially assist the reader of the works thus mentioned.

J.

English Romance. So constant is the appearance of new novels, and so confirmed appears to be the appetite for them, that it seems useless to remonstrate ; but it may be feared that no good account can be given to God for much time employed in reading them. Yet there are novels in our language which ought to be read, as an accompaniment to other books. Nearly the whole of them may be named within the compass of this note; and wisely distributed as helps to other reading, they may be of real service.

Such a story as *Robinson Crusoe* cannot be too highly estimated, as tending to open the mind and enlarge the ideas of a growing boy; and when the study of history is fairly inaugurated, such stories as *Ivanhoe*, and *Quentin Durward*, will also have a beneficial influence. When a youth is disposed to read *Kenilworth*, let him reflect that it portrays the lighter features of the age succeeding the Reformation; and the *Fortunes of Nigel* may be safely read by one who sees in it the manners of that epoch to which we owe our common English Bible. *Woodstock* must be dignified by association with the trials and troubles of the Church of England, under the Commonwealth. *The Vicar of Wakefield* may be read in maturer youth, as a picture of the times which succeeded the accession of the House of Hanover; and, as it is really important that society in England, in our own times, should be comprehended, it may be well, with books of travel, to read such a work as *Ten Thousand a Year*, by Mr. Warren. As for the fashionable low-life novels, of the sentimental and cynical sort, it is a pity that they should find any favour with Christians; and the reading of popular novels of the sensual French school, should be regarded as a positive immorality.

There are two novels, which need only to be furnished with proper notes and comments, to be of great value to the young Christian who would learn something of the state of society before and after the nominal conversion of the Roman Empire. Each is disfigured by great blemishes, yet they have great merits. I refer to Bulwer's *Last Days of Pompeii*, and Kingsley's *Hypatia*. The former is feeble in its attempted portraiture of the early Christian martyrs. The latter does little justice to the nobler features of a critical period in the history of the Church; yet it shows forcibly the evil of those terrible conflicts of popular feeling which necessarily followed the breaking up of old systems and superstitions, while the masses were yet undisciplined by the faith which they had only in form embraced.

K.

Theological Literature. To this study we possess an introduction, in an admirable popular form, in the two volumes entitled
The Literature of the Church of England, by the Rev. R. Cattermole, B. D. Though published in England, the work is in the mar-
ket, at a very low price, and it ought to be generally circulated.
Wilberforce's *Five Empires,* and also *The Manual of Church
History,* by Palmer (edited by Bishop Whittingham), should be in
every library; as also Wordsworth's *Theophilus Anglicanus,*
edited by H. D. Evans, Esq. The work of Dr. Evans on *Anglican
Ordinations,* is not only a refutation of the pretences and imputa-
tions of Romish writers, but it also contains much valuable information, not elsewhere to be found, on many subordinate points. To
this, the same author's Essay on the *American Episcopate* is an important supplement.

L.

The Poetry of Spenser. At the well-head of "English undefiled,"
we have a noble Church-poet, who celebrates, in the Red-Cross
Knight, the achievements of Faith. In the artful but foul Duessa
he gives a just portrait of Romanism, and in the pure and heavenly-
minded Una, he displays the primitive charms of the Anglican
Church.

The *Minor Poems* of Milton are almost all conceived in the spirit
of his Church-education; and nowhere is Puritanism betrayed in
those parts of Paradise Lost which are attractive, and meritorious
as poetry. He justly eulogized Jeremy Taylor as the Father of
Religious Toleration, and stigmatized the Puritans as his persecutors
and as the enemies of religious liberty, in his poem on the *New
Forcers of Conscience,* etc. In general, the poetry of our language
may be regarded as wholly ours.

But the young will generally form their taste, in poetry, by inti-
macy with contemporary authors. Happily the reigning poets,
Tennyson and Longfellow, are such as they may safely read. To
the latter we owe a debt for the elevation he has given to the tastes
of our countrymen, and for the general harmony of his thought and
expression with what is Church-like. In so sacred a task as I am
now performing, however, candor compels me to remind parents
and instructors that the morality and religion of even Mr. Long-

fellow's charming poetry are not free from somewhat of indefiniteness and indifferentism, though in a very refined and subtle form. What is *picturesque*, rather than what is real and truthful, is, no doubt unconsciously, worked into many of his poems, on a principle of eclecticism which is dangerous to the youthful mind. Such a mosaic is not without a pleasing general effect, and has a sort of beauty, till one discovers that the *undique collata membra* belong in parts to Luther, Calvin, and the Pope, and make up the Horatian monster—

> " ——————— ut turpiter atrum
> Desinat in piscem mulier formosa superne."

In some of our American writers, what Mr. Longfellow so refines and spiritualizes, usually goes on the ground, and eats dirt without disguise. " Jehovah, Jove, or Lord," is the only creed of many popular authors, and a debased morality is the inevitable consequence. Of this we have an extreme instance in the unhappy Poe, who seems never to have conceived of any such idea as that of the truth. Shelley and Byron, whom he imitates in a coarse way, pay tribute to the Church and to the literature of our language, so far as they show that they are quite conscious of their rebellion against a pure morality and a definite doctrinal Christianity ; but of Poe it must be said that he seems wholly ignorant that sin is not virtue, and that blasphemy is not adoration. This is the level to which the numerous godless schools and colleges of America are fast degrading us. Oh ! that authors of the nobler sort would—

> " *Rise* to truth, and moralize their song,"

and so contribute something to the arrest of that national corruption to which all things gravitate rapidly. Or, are we doomed to see a revolt of the minds and consciences of our countrymen from all recognized standards of truth and right ?

The poetry of Wordsworth and Southey cannot be too freely used in education. The *Ecclesiastical Sketches* of the former should be read with Southey's *Book of the Church*. Bishop Mant's *Sonnets* are not unworthy of particular mention.

M.

Benefactors. The names of these three Christian heroes—Bray, Blair, and Berkeley—would be as familiarly known as those of

Lafayette, Kosciusko, and Pulaski, if our countrymen were wont to estimate moral benefits as justly as they do the services of our military allies. For the most accessible information concerning their disinterested and self-sacrificing lives, consult Sprague's " Annals."

N.

Berkeley. Among Mr. Tuckerman's interesting "Biographical Essays" will be found one on Bishop Berkeley, well worthy of being read. Everybody knows his noble verses "On planting Letters in America." May his generous predictions be realized!

O.

Milton. At the early age of three-and-thirty, Milton undertook to match himself with the giants of intellect and learning who were then ranged on the Church's side, "being willing," he says, "to *help the Puritans,* who were inferior to the prelates in learning." But in this attempt he seems to have felt his own failure, for he acknowledges himself "not disposed to this manner of writing," and adds, "wherein knowing myself inferior to myself, led by the genial power of nature to another task, I have the use, as I may account it, *but of my left hand.*" In other words, in his Puritanism he did violence to his genius, and made a left-hand marriage, the fruit of which has been his lasting reproach.

P.

Suggestion. We need new editions of *The Scholar Armed,* Law's *Letters to the Bishop of Bangor,* Leslie's *Short Method,* Waterland's *Regeneration and Justification,* Scott's *Christian Life,* and other old-fashioned Church-books, which contributed greatly to the forming of our earlier American Churchmen.

Q.

Anecdote. An eminent Presbyterian divine once remarked, in the author's hearing, that "nothing but his conscientious convictions could keep him out of a Church which belongs to the history of the race, and which is identified with the Literature of our mother tongue." He felt it to be a misfortune that he could not conform; and in this confession, if he paid a just tribute to the Church, he did honour to himself, not only as making sacrifices to his honest views of duty, but as having the elevated taste and mental power to appreciate the vast advantages, which Churchmen possess in this ennobling inheritance.

R.

Resources. The publications of the Christian Knowledge Society many of which are very desirable, may now be ordered through our society. A moment's comparison of its catalogues with those of any of our Mixed Societies, will enable any one to see for himself the advantage possessed by it, as being entirely under the control of the Church, and so enabled to reproduce standard works without mutilation. The Bible Commentary of D'Oyly and Mant, in three imperial octavos, beautifully printed on linen paper, and illustrated with maps (it contains also the Apocrypha), may be had, at a very low price, from the press of the C. K. S., and it ought to be found in every family library. It would be a good thing if Bishop Hobart's valuable additions to this Commentary might be incorporated with the English edition.

S.

Decline of Morals. The tendency of our popular literature has been to Germanize education in our country, rather than to make it emulate the system of Eton and Oxford, or the Rugby system, so happily illustrated by the author of *Tom Brown's School-days.* Had Irving's influence been unchecked by that of others, we should have found our young men in colleges taking as naturally to caps and gowns, and cricket and chess, as they now do to the *meerschaum* and blouses ; and as willing to imitate the May-day hymn on Magdalen Tower as they now are to keep up the *Gaudeamus igitur,* with all the accompaniments of a Heidelberg dehauch. The consequences of our low college-morals may be seen in Congress, and everywhere else, among those who rank as educated men. Where now do we see the manners of Hamilton and Jay, and of the elder statesmen of Virginia? We have every reason to fear that this Germanizing mania will not long forbear to introduce the duelling and other customs of the Rhine-land, by which the *bursch* is distinguished from the *fuchs.* The only resource of parents is to be found in our rising Church-colleges.

40

T.

English Literature our Own. I quote the author to whom I have referred, as follows :

"Whether we will or no, the phraseology and diction of Shakspeare, of *the Protestant formularies*"—he means the Bible and Prayer-book—" of Milton, of Pope, of Johnson's Table-talk, and of Walter Scott, have become *a portion of the vernacular tongue ;* the household words of which, perhaps, we little guess the origin, and the very idioms of our familiar conversation. . . . . *So tyrannous is the literature of a nation ; it is too much for us.* We cannot destroy or reverse it. . . . . English literature will ever have been Protestant;" by which he means Anglican. " Swift and Addison, the most native and natural of our writers, Hooker and Milton, the most elaborate, never can become our co-religionists."—Newman's "University Subjects," p. 91.

Let these remarks of one who has sold his birthright, be considered in connection with the principles of this sermon, and let us do all in our power to make the literature of America " too much for them ;"—I mean Jesuits and Liguorians. It is worth adding, that Mr. Newman's vast superiority to all those who surround him, and who were trained as Romanists, demonstrates the greatness of these blessings of his former lot, for which he makes such ungrateful returns to man and to his God.

U.

The Six Principles. This has been shown more fully by Bishop Potter, in his remarks on the S. S. Union, published with the essay on "Mixed Societies," by the author of this sermon

V.

The Probable Future. If the reading of a youth, in Yale College, in the year 1720, when the Church had hardly any real existence in the land, has resulted in the founding of such a Church as now exists in the diocese of Connecticut (and that in spite of the strong hold which the Puritans then had upon the whole of New-England), what may not be the result, by the blessing of God, on the labours of this Society, in our West and elsewhere, under an efficient episcopate, and with the means we now possess to enlarge our work ? The reader is referred to the Life of Dr. Johnson, in Sprague's " Annals."

This allusion to New-Haven reminds the author that a closing word is due to our periodical literature, and to the claims of the *Church Review*, published in that city. Considering the great obstacles encountered by Dr. Richardson, its editor, in the establishment and support of such a work, he deserves very high praise for the length of time during which he has kept it up, and for the amount of ability with which it is sustained. Every family should be supplied, in addition to a well-selected Church newspaper, with such a guide to intelligent opinion upon contemporary subjects. In conclusion, the author would express his hope that the admirable papers of H. D. Evans, Esq., for so many years contributed to the *True Catholic*, and so commendable for profound thought, as well as for a singular perspicuity and propriety of style, may soon be collected, and made a permanent portion of the growing wealth of our American Church.

W.

SUGGESTIONS FOR A LIBRARY.—With the kind assistance of several friends, I have thrown together a list of the works which are likely to be found most useful in parochial and domestic libraries. In country parishes much good might be done by the *union of families*, each family agreeing to purchase a select portion from this list, (so that nearly all might be found in the town or village,) and to lend mutually, on terms and for times pre-arranged. Those works marked (*a*) with an Alpha, are such as have been approved by the Committee of General Literature.

A moment's glance at this list will suggest to the critic many objections. It enumerates some works that are rather professional than popular: some that are liable to censure on this ground or that; and it omits many that are useful and important to a Parish Library, if not to a domestic one. Further, it is not carefully arranged, much less digested into a plan so as to exhibit comparative merit. All this is true—and it is equally true, notwithstanding, that it is a list on which all the time and thought possible (amid other engagements, and while these sheets were passing the press) have been expended. There are reasons for omissions and for insertions, which have suggested themselves, but which it would be tedious to express. Suffice it, that a judicious pastor, by the use of his lead-pencil, may, with this help, direct the attention of a parishioner in a few minutes, to many books suitable for his reading, which might otherwise be overlooked. Popular books are at everybody's hand, and we need not put them into such a record. Of this class, such as are here specified are those about which there can be no doubt that they supply a popular necessity not otherwise met. It is to be hoped that an approved list, well arranged, and as full as possible, may soon be issued by the Church Book Society.

1. Biblical.

a Doyly and Mant's Commentary.
a Plain Commentary on the Gospels.
a " " " Psalms.
Hall's Notes on the Gospels.
English Harmony in Paragraphs and Parallelisms. (Parker, Oxford.)
Hawkins' Psalter.
Westcott's History of the Canon.
Goulbourne's Lectures on Inspiration.
Paley's Horæ Paulinæ.
a Conybeare and Howson's St. Paul.
Anderson's Annals of the English Bible.
Lee's Inspiration of Scripture.
Williams' Study of the Gospels.
Westcott's Principles of the Harmony.
Jones' Figurative Language of Scripture.
Bp. Hall's Explication of Hard Texts.
Sumner's Practical Reflections.
a Trench on Miracles.
a " " Parables.
Horne'e Introduction.
Nichol's Help to Study of the Bible.

2. Devotional.

a Whole Duty of Man.
Scongal's Life of God in the Soul.
a Wilson's Sacra Privata. (Denton's new Edition.)

Hobart's (Bp.) Christian Manual.
Andrewes' Preces Privatæ, or Devotions.
Hobart's (J. H.) Instructions for Lent.
Kip's Lenten Fast.
Sutton's Disce Vivere and Disce Mori.
a Taylor's Holy Living and Dying, and Golden Grove.
Spincke's Devotions.
Law's Serious Call.
Sherlock's Practical Christian.
Patrick's Parable of the Pilgrim.
" Repentance and Fasting.
" on Prayer.
" Advice to a Friend.
a Mant's Happiness of the Blessed.

3. Theological.

McIlvaine's Evidences.
Wordsworth's Christian Institutes.
Kaye's Tertullian.
" Justin Martyr.
" Clement of Alexandria.
Butler's Analogy.
" Ethical Sermons. (Passmore's Edition.)
Sewell's Christian Morals.
Shuttleworth's Consistency of Revelation, (Harper's edition.)
Leighton's Works

Taylor's Works. (Several cheap edi-
tions.)
Barrow's Works.
Horne's Works.
Tyrrell on the Ritual.
Mant's Holy-Days.
Nelson's Festivals and Fasts.
Staunton's Church Dictionary.
Hook's   "   "
Dorr's Churchman's Manual.
a Browne on the Articles.
a Pearson on the Creed.
a Brownell on the Common Prayer.
a Wheatley   "   "   "
  Humphrey "   "   "
a Hallam on the Morning Prayer.
  Procter's History of the Common
  Prayer.
a Blunt's Undesigned Coincidences.
a Blunt's Parish Priest.
  Tyler's Primitive Worship.
  Hind's Progress of Christianity.
  Burton's Divinity of Christ.
  "   "   the Holy Ghost.
a Faber's Difficulties of Infidelity.
  "   "   Romanism.
a Moberly's Great Forty Days.
a Kip's Double-Witness.
  Waterland on the Athanasian Creed.
  (C. K. S. Edition.)
  Bp. Hopkins' (Vermont) Letters to
  Kenrick, and other Works.
  Butler's (W. A.) Letters on Romanism.
  Scudamore's England and Rome.
  Wordsworth on the Apocalypse.
  Lay's (Bp.) Tracts for Missionary Use.
a Morgan on Infidelity.
  Craik's Search of Truth.
  Wilson's Church Identified.
  Leslie's Short Method with Deists.

Faber's Primitive Doctrine of Election.
Macdonnel on the Atonement.
Jerram on Infant Baptism.
Wall's History of Infant Baptism.
Hussey's Rise of the Papal Power.
Palmer's Letters to Wiseman.
Theophilus Americanus. (Evans'.)
Laborde on the Immaculate Concep-
tion. (Translation.)
Jarvis' Church of the Redeemed.
Gifford's Unison of the Liturgy.
West on the Resurrection.
Hobart's State of the Departed.
Adams' Christian Science.
"   Mercy to Babes.
Bp. Bull's Vindication of the Church
of England. (Balt. Edition.)
Vincent of Lerins. ("   )
Wilson's English Reformation.
"   Church Principles.
Lawrence's Bampton Lectures.
Bethell on Regeneration.
Palmer on Romanism.
Rome's Moral Theology. (Meyrick.
Balt. Edition.)
Evans' Anglican Ordinations. (Balt.
Edition.)
Cosin's History of Transubstantiation.
Beaven's Intercourse between the
Church of England and the Churches
of the East.
Southgate's Syrian Churches.
Barrow on the Pope's Supremacy.
Wake's Apostolic Fathers.
Kaye's (Bp.) Government and Disci
pline of the Church.
Miss Sewell's Readings for Every Day
in Lent.
Miss Sewell's Readings for a Month be-
fore Confirmation.

Daubeny's Guide to the Church.
Jones on the Trinity.
Waterland on the Trinity.

4. Sermons.

a W. Archer Butler's Sermons.
Melville's   "
Le Bas'   "
Bp. Armstrong's   "
Monroe's   "
Ninety Short Sermons.
Sermons for the Seasons. (Parker's Ed.)
Barrow's Sermons.
Bp. Sanderson's Sermons.
Wainwright's   "
Horne's   "
Porteus'   "
Bp. Dehon's   "
Horsley's   "
Chapman's Sermons on the Church.
Heber's Sermons.
Dr. Lewis' Sermons.

5. History.

Annals of England, 3 vols. Parker, Oxford.
a Churton's Early English Church.
a Soames's Anglo-Saxons.
a Palgrave's Anglo-Saxons.
   Dr. Coit's Lectures on Early English Church.
a Massingberd's Reformation.
a Palmer's History of the Church.
   Russell's History of the Church of Scotland.
   Turner's Sacred History of the World.
   Wilberforce's Five Empires.
   Cave's Primitive Christianity.
a Anderson's Church of England in the Colonies.

Badger's Nestorians and their Ritual.
Bates' Christian Antiquities.
Bingham's Christian Antiquities, 2 vols. (cheap Bungay Ed.)
Eusebius' Eccl. History. (Translation.)
   "   Life of Constantine. (Translation. Bohn's Ed.)
Miller's Philosophy of History.
Tytler's History of Scotland.
Smedley's Sketches from Venetian History.
Smedley's Hist. of the Church of France.
Neale's Eastern Church.
Mouravieff's Russian Church.
Anjou's (Mason's Translation) Swedish Church.
Riddle's Manual of Christian Antiquities.
Blunt's Sketch of the Reformation.
a Southey's Book of the Church.
a Fuller's Church History.
a Clarendon's History of the Rebellion.
a Burnet's Own Times.
a D'Israeli's Charles I.
a Evelyn's Diary and Letters.
a Carwithen's History of the Church of England.
   Coit's Puritanism.
   Bp. White's Memoirs of American Church.
   Spencer's (J. A.) Reformation.
a Robertson's First Five Centuries.
a Hardwicke's Reformation.
a   "   Middle Ages.
   Blunt's (J. J.) Five Lectures on the Church in the First Two Centuries.
   Blunt's Study of the Fathers.
   Poole's Life and Times of St. Cyprian.
   Russell's Connection of Sacred and Profane Literature.

6. Biography.

Cave's Lives of the Apostles.
"   "   "   Fathers.
R. W. Evans' Biography of the Early Church.
Hook's Ecclesiastical Biography
Rose's Biographical Dictionary.
Chandler's Life of Wykeham.
a Le Bas'   "   " Wiclif.
u   "   "   " Cranmer.
u   "   "   Laud.
Le Bas' Life of Jewel.
a Walton's Lives.
Heber's Life of Jeremy Taylor.
Nelson's Life of Bp. Bull.
Patrick's (Bp.) Autobiography.
Burgon's Life of Sir T. Gresham.
"   "   " P. F. Tytler.
Johnson's Lives of the Poets.
a Boswell's Life of Johnson. (Illustrated. 12mo. London.)
Tytler's (P. F.) Life of Sir Walter Raleigh.
Southey's Life of Wesley.
Wilberforce's Life and Letters.
Wordsworth's "   "   "
Hannah More's Life and Letters.
Prichard's Life of Anselm.
Prior's Life of Burke.
Tytler's Lives of Scottish Worthies.
Wordsworth's Ecclesiastical Biography
Evans' (R. W.) Scripture Biography.
Caswall's Life of Leacock (Martyr of the Pongas.)
E. D. Griffin's Remains.
B. D. Winslow's Remains.
T. W. Eastburn's   "
Wolfe's   "
McVickar's Hobart.
a Fuller's Worthies.

Herbert's Two Last Years of Charles I.
a Burnet's Lives. (Jebb's Edition.)
Sprague's (Fifth Volume) Annals.
a Heber's Life and Journals, by his Widow.
Last Days of Bp. Heber.
Bp. Chase's Reminiscences.
Life of Bishop White. (Wilson.)
"   " Suckling.
a "   " Headley Vicars.
Life of Thos. Cole, by Noble.
Life of John Howard.
Southey's Life of Cowper.
a Life of Henry Martin. (Thomason.)
Life of Bishop Armstrong.
"   Robert Nelson.

7. Poetry.

a Herbert's Poems.
a Keble's Christian Year.
Lyra Apostolica.
a Wordsworth's Works.
a Southey's Works.
Spenser's Faery-Queen.
Herrick's Noble Numbers.
Wiffen's Tasso.
Cary's Dante.
H. K. White's Works.
Bp. Heber's Poems.
Cowper's Poems.
. Mrs. Hemans' Poems.
Hillhouse's Poems.
a Bp. Mant's Sonnets.
Bowles' Sonnets.
Mrs. Southey's Poems.
Lyra Germanica.
Christmas with the Poets.
Thomson's Seasons.
Goldsmith's Poems.
Crabbe's Poems.
Cleveland Psalter.

Keble's Psalter.
Burgess' (Bp. of Maine) Psalter.
Dr. Muhlenberg's Poems.
Croswell's Poems.   (In press.)
Clement C. Moore's Poems.
R. H. Dana's Poems.
Doane's Poems.   (In press.)

8. Miscellany.

Addison's Works.
Johnson's   "
Burke's Works.
Bacon's Essays.
Beveridge's Private Thoughts.
Brown's (Sir Thomas) Works.
a Walton's Angler.
Cecil's Remains.
Edmonson's Christian Gentleman.
De Foe's Journal of the Plague.
Irving's Works.
Verplanck's Essays.
a Kip's Early Conflicts of Christianity.
a "   Christmas Holidays in Rome.
a "   Catacombs.
Lander's Expedition on the Niger.
Coleridge's Aids to Reflection. (McVick-
    ar's.)
Coleridge's (Bp.) Six Months in West-
    Indies.
Gleig's History of British India.
Jebb's Correspondence.
Prichard's Natural History of Man.
Mudie's Birds.
White's Selborne.
Russell's Palestine.
    "   Nubia and Abyssinia.
Russell's Egypt.
Caswall's Church in America.
    "   Western World Revisited.
    "   Church in Scotland.

Paget's Tales.
Gresley's Tales.
Feltham's Resolves.
Goldsmith's Vicar of Wakefield.
a Records of a Good Man's Life.
Rectory of Valehead.
Scenes in Our Parish.
a Herbert's Country Parson.
Tracts for the Christian Seasons.
Palgrave's Merchant and Friar.
Bloxam's Gothic Architecture.
Glossary of Architecture. (Parker, Ox-
    ford.)
Barr's Anglican Architecture.
Calendar of the Anglican Church Il-
    lustrated.
Markland on English Churches.
Cattermole's Literature of the Church
    of England.
a Reed's Lectures on English History.
a "   "   "   "   Literature.
a Hudson's Lectures on Shakespeare.
a Buchanan's Researches.
B. Montague's Selections from Old Eng-
    lish Divines.
Spencer's Selections from Old English
    Divines.
Dean Trench's Works.
Warburton's Crescent and Cross.
Luther's Table Talk.
Neale's Latin Hymns.
Layard's Nineveh.
Cattermole's Sacred Poetry of the
    XVII. Century.
Mrs. Southey's Chapters on Church-
    yards.
Selections from Hooker.
Bp. Andrewe's Select Works.
Bp. Wilson's   "   "

Sonth's Select Works,
Bp. Psarson's "
Jones (of Nayland) Letters of a Tutor.
  "   "   Book of Nature.
Bell on the Hand.
Rogst's Bridgewater Treatise.
Hervey's Book of Christmas.
Thomas à Kempis.
a Pascal's Thoughts and Provincial Letters.
St. Augustine's Confessions.
Cooper's (Miss) Rural Hours.
Willmott's (R. A.) Summer Time in the Country.

Legion, or Feigned Excuses, by Leakin,
Legh Richmond's Works.
Practical Christian's Library. (Selections from Old Divines.)
Half-Hours with the Best Authors.
Letters of Wm. Cowper.
Evans' Tales of the Ancient British Church.
Maxims of Washington (Schroeder's.)
The East, Sketches of Travel in Egypt and the Holy Land, By J. A. Spencer, D. D.
Heber's Journey through India.
Bishop Wainwright's Travels.

X.

CORROBORATIONS.—While these pages were detained in the hands of the printer, new signs of the times have been supplying evidence of the views I have endeavoured to support, concerning the mission of the Church, amid the manifold sectarianism of America. The Romanists, by the political manifesto of "nine bishops," have thrown off the mask, and allied themselves, *openly*, with the spirit of arbitrary power, and confessed that the *temporal* as well as the *spiritual* claims of the Pope are virtually part of their religion. On the other hand, the *New-York Observer*, a prominent organ of popular religion, informs us that "not a week passes without fresh evidence of a lamentable defection from the truth on the part of some of the ministers and churches in New-England." The late movement among Unitarians shows that a reaction is beginning among them, and that the Church is manifesting itself more and more to earnest and reflecting minds, as the only resource of a healthful and genuine loyalty to Christ.

To such minds, therefore, we commend a re-examination of the English Reformation, believing that it may lead them to more just ideas of the true character of that Church from which their fathers broke off in a spirit of rash, though conscientious, experiment.

And as introductory to such researches, we ask the considerate reading of the following paragraph from Dr. Tulloch, (an eminent divine of the Kirk of Scotland,) on the spirit of the Church of England, as contrasted with the individualism and consequent narrowness of Sect. Although there are expressions in it which mark it as written by a Presbyterian, it is, nevertheless, such a candid and generous tribute to the Church of the Anglo-Saxon race, that it must be read with benefit by any one.

"From the beginning this Church repudiated the distinct guidance of any theoretical principles, however exalted and apparently Scriptural. It held fast to its historical position, as a great Institute, still living and powerful under all the corruptions which had overlaid it; and while submitting to the irresistible influence of reform which swept over it, as over other Churches in the sixteenth century, it refused to be refashioned according to any new model. It broke away from the medieval bondage, under which it had always been restless, and destroyed the gross abuses which had sprung out of it; it rose in attitude of proud and successful resistance to Rome; but in doing all this, it did not go to Scripture, *as if it had once more, and entirely anew, to find there the principles either of doctrinal truth or practical government and discipline. Scripture indeed was eminently the condition of its revival; but Scripture was not made anew the foundation of its existence.* There was too much of old historical life in it to seek any new foundation : the new must grow out of the old, and fit itself into the old. The Church of England was to be reformed, but not reconstituted. *Its life was too vast ; its influence too varied ; its relations too complicated*—touching the national existence in all its multiplied expressions, at too many points—*to be capable of being reduced to any new* and definite form in more *supposed* uniformity with the model of Scripture, or the simplicity of the Primitive Church. Its extensive and manifold organism was to be reanimated by new life, but not remoulded according to any arbitrary or novel theory..... ...The spirit, at once progressive and conservative, comprehensive rather than intensive, historical and not dogmatical, is one eminently characteristic of the English mind, and as it appears to us, in the highest degree characteristic of the English Reformation."